Allen the Alligator

Written & Illustrated

By Sami Holt

Inspired by:
Nora Grotha
aka Granny

In a small home off Springfield street,

Allen the Alligator has lived.

His own slice of heaven,

or so he believed.

Just around the corner,

and over the bridge.

He enjoyed the peace and quiet,
of his very own acreage.

Here he loved being outside,

just away from the crowd.

This was a big deal,
which made Allen feel so proud.

There he built a large garden,

at the side of his yard.

Working day in and out,

no doubt he worked hard.

The work kept him strong,

but so did the vegetables.

STRONG

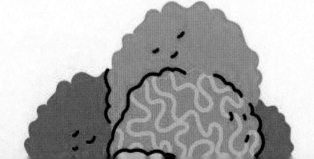

Try eating your veggies too,

if you are so skeptical….

He would plant many veggies,

and bright flowers of course.

Just ask the birds,

they're his very best source.

Especially the cardinals,

whose singing fills his heart.

Working alongside one another,

they are never far apart.

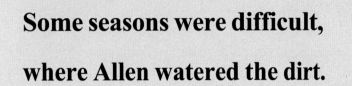

Some seasons were difficult,

where Allen watered the dirt.

Others were rewarding,

and the earth covered his shirt.

Earning Garden of the Month,

it was believed his thumb was green.

When the night's get colder,

Allen will need to be prepared.

But he isn't worried,

as food is meant to be shared.

With tons of food to harvest still,

he would soon run out of space.

But Allen the Alligator was smart,

all the produce wouldn't be stored at his place.

He would share with his friends,

and his neighbors too.

So, nothing would go to waste,

well, maybe just a few.

**When the gardening was done,
and winter weather was in the air.**

Allen would enjoy the warmth,
and watch the seasons change from his chair

If he needed a snack,

he wouldn't need to go far.

Allen could go to his pantry,

where his veggies were canned in a jar.

If there is something you can learn,

from Allen the Alligator thus far.

It's to find joy in the things you choose to do,

and always be confident in who you are.

Made in the USA
Monee, IL
03 March 2023

28694775R00021